WEB OF FRIENDSHIP

Adapted by Michael Teitelbaum

based on the Digimon episode
"Arukenimon's Tangled Web"

by Becky Olkowsky and
Jeff Nimoy & Bob Buchholz

SCHOLASTIC INC.

New York Toronto London Auckland Sydney
Mexico City New Delhi Hong Kong Buenos Aires

Three friends named Davis, Cody Hida, and Ken Ichijoji were exploring the Digital World. They came upon a giant house, bigger than any house they had ever seen.

"I wonder what is inside," Cody said.

Davis, Ken, and Cody stepped inside.

"Everything is so huge!" Ken said. "I feel like an insect."

The three friends climbed up a kitchen cabinet.

"This is like climbing a mountain!" Davis said.

After a hard climb, Ken, Davis, and Cody finally reached the top of the cabinet. Standing on the counter, they heard strange music.

"Someone is playing a flute," Cody said, looking around. "But I cannot see anyone."

Suddenly, hundreds of insect Digimon crawled out of the drain in the kitchen sink.

The insect Digimon raced onto the counter, heading right for Ken, Davis, and Cody.

"Run!" Davis shouted.
The three friends dashed along the counter. The insect Digimon chased them.

Cody spotted Arukenimon, the evil witch. She sat on a windowsill, playing her magic flute.

"The music from her flute must be controlling the insect Digimon," Cody explained. "She is making them attack us!"

The three friends were so worried about the insect Digimon that they did not notice they had reached the end of the counter. They tumbled over the edge..

Cody, Ken, and Davis landed
in a giant spiderweb!

"I am stuck to the web!" Ken shouted.

"Me too!" Davis yelled.

"How are we going to get out of here?" Cody wondered.

Arukenimon looked down at the trapped boys. Then she began playing her magic flute again.

Davis, Cody, and Ken struggled to free themselves from the spiderweb.

"This is why I do not surf the Internet," Davis said. "I hate web sites! Especially ones that I am stuck to!"

A giant spider began climbing up the web, heading right for the three friends.

"It is Dokugumon!" Cody cried. "Arukenimon must have called him with her magic flute."

"Unfortunately for us," Ken said, "I think it is his feeding time!"

"My hands are stuck to the web!" Davis cried. "So are mine!" Ken said. "And Dokugumon keeps getting closer! Cody, do you have any ideas about how we can escape?"

"We are all ears, Cody,"
Davis said. "But you better
think fast!"

Cody thought quickly. He had to come up with a plan.

He looked around and saw an air conditioner on the wall above the spiderweb.

Then Cody spotted a rock that was stuck in the web near Ken's feet. "I have an idea!" Cody said.

"We can get out of here if we work together as a team," Cody explained. "Just like when we play soccer in the real world."

The giant spider crept closer and closer to the three friends.

"What do you mean, Cody?" Davis asked.

"Ken, use that rock near your feet like a soccer ball!" Cody shouted. "Pass it to Davis."

"What good will that do?" Davis asked.

"If we can hit the button that turns on that air conditioner, maybe we can blow Dokugumon off the web," Cody explained.

"Great!" Davis shouted. "Ken, pass that rock over here!"

Ken reached out with his feet and grabbed the rock. Using all his strength, he tossed the rock into the air.

The rock flew through the air toward Davis. Davis kicked the rock, directing it toward the air conditioner. "Just like playing soccer back home!" Davis said.

The rock soared high into the air. It struck a button that turned on the air conditioner.

The force of the blowing air pushed against Dokugumon. He struggled to stay on the web. But the powerful blast of air knocked him right off.

As he fell, Dokugumon grabbed for the web. His sharp claws tore the web to shreds.

With the web destroyed, Cody, Davis, and Ken tumbled gently to the floor. They landed safely and scrambled to their feet.

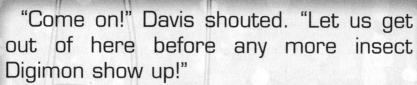

"Come on!" Davis shouted. "Let us get out of here before any more insect Digimon show up!"

The three friends raced from the house.

"Nice plan, Cody," Ken said when they got outside. "It really saved us."

"Nice kick, Davis," Cody replied.

"Nice teamwork, guys," Davis said. "But the next time we find a giant house, I think we should just look at it from the outside!"